D0293297

Praise for Boing-Boing the Bionic Cat

"Boing-Boing is a small furry feline who has saved the Natural History Museum from a jewel thief, an Egyptologist from the Mummy's Revenge ... and has made thousands of children laugh – Boing-Boing, bionic cat and superhero."

Evening Standard

"This one of a kind eccentric and intriguing picture book tells the story of Daniel who cannot have a pet because he is allergic to cats. Enter Professor George who is inspired by the challenge of creating a bionic cat. The right reader/listener will be mesmerised by this glimpse into the world of robot engineering."

Parent's Choice Magazine

"Boing-Boing is a welcome relief to the majority of children's science books."

21st Century Science

Boing-Boing

the bionic cat
and the space station

Written by Larry L. Hench

Illustrations by Tom Morgan-Jones

Published by The Can of Worms Kids Press

Boing-Boing the Bionic Cat
and the Space Station

Written by Larry L. Hench
Illustrations by Tom Morgan-Jones

Published by Can of Worms Kids Press
7 Peacock Yard
London SE17 3LH
United Kingdom

Telephone: +44 (0)20 7708 2942
E-mail: info@canofwormsenterprises.co.uk
Web site: www.canofwormsenterprises.co.uk

Printed in Poland
Design by Helen Steer and Emily Atkins
Cover by Helen Steer

A CIP catalogue record for this book is available from the British Library
ISBN: 978-1-904872-07-8

Images on pages 71-72, 73-74, 81-82 and 83-84 copyright © NASA/courtesy of
nasaimages.org

Being friendly to our environment
We take being friendly to our planet seriously. No animals were hurt in the making
of this book and we have been very careful with how we use trees. We have only
used paper certified by the Forest Stewardship Council.

A few more words on recycling
All the words in Boing-Boing have been recycled. You will have seen most of them
elsewhere but if not you can find them in a dictionary or for some of the especially
difficult words in this book in the glossary at the end. Please feel free to send us any
words you might wish to at: info@canofwormsenterprises.co.uk

Daniel, Jessica, Jennifer, Elliot, James, Robert
and especially June

Professor George says...

Dear Readers,

Thank you for joining Daniel and me on this new Boing-Boing adventure. For this mission into space I have implanted sharp silicon carbide claws into Boing-Boing's paws. *Boing-Boing the Bionic Cat and the Space Station* is the sixth book in our series of adventures and the first time a bionic cat has left the Earth's orbit. Read on and enjoy, and if you've not read the first five books check out the back of this book where you can see what else Boing-Boing has been up to.

Parents and Teachers: While these books have been written for fun, they have also been adopted by schools to help teach children about science and technology. In the Boing-Boing series the general synopsis of the books is as follows: Daniel, who loves cats but is allergic to them, is delighted when his inventive neighbor Professor George – that's me, an engineer – builds him a bionic cat with fibre-optic fur, computer-controlled joints, electronic eyes, and ceramic-sensor whiskers. It's just like a real cat, but Daniel is not allergic to it! With each succeeding adventure I add new technological features to Boing-Boing. Everything that I make Boing-Boing do in this book can be done at home or at school.

Glossary: You will see some words highlighted in bold. These words may be difficult for some readers to understand, so at the end of this book you will find a glossary explaining their meanings.

If you have any questions about Boing-Boing, please do not hesitate to write to me by e-mail: professor.george@boing-boing.org or by post: Professor George, c/o Can of Worms Kids Press, 7 Peacock Yard, Illife Street, London, SE17 3LH, United Kingdom.

Contents

Bionic Cat

Bionic Eyes
(optical sensors that detect light,
dark, infrared and motion)

Bionic Ears
(sound sensors that respond
to voice commands from
Daniel and send electrical
signals to the computer)

Bionic Whiskers
(piezoelectric ceramics
on the end of metallic
conductors that convert
heat, pressure, and
mechanical deflection
into electrical signals)

On-Off Button
(activates electrical
power to the computer
and bionic parts)

Bionic Tail
(four multi-axial
joints that enable
tail to move in all
directions under
computer control)

Computer
(small, powerful, programmable
microprocessor that converts
electrical signals from sensors
to control bionic legs, tail, head,
and voice box)

Gyroscope
(rapid rotation of spinning disc
provides input to the computer
to maintain orientation while
climbing or falling)

design features

Batteries
(six rechargeable 9-volt batteries that provide power to the computer, the bionic eyes, tail, legs, head, and ceramic heating elements)

Fibre-Optic Fur
(optical glass fibre, covering all surfaces, that transmits sunlight through the fibres to photovoltaic cells that charge the batteries)

Bionic Tail Sensor
(piezoelectric ceramic sensor in tail joint that sends signals to the computer and voice simulator to generate a ROAR with the loudness increasing as pressure on the sensor increases)

Bionic Legs
(four legs with three multi-axial joints per leg connected to small motors controlled by the computer)

Bionic Claws
(retractable hard and sharp silicon carbide ceramic)

Bionic Voice Box
(programmable voice simulator activated by sensors embedded in the fibre-optic fur; controlled by the computer)

chapter one

aniel looked up and saw his bionic cat crawling along one of the top branches, his fibre-optic fur shining in the sunlight.

"What's he doing up there? Why doesn't he fall?" asked Amy as Boing-Boing swung upside down and hung on the branch.

"Boing-Boing is trying to get my plane that landed in the tree," replied Daniel. "See the red wing on the branch just below Boing-Boing? He's almost got it."

"But Danny, how can he do that without falling?" asked Amy again.

"Remember, Amy," answered Daniel, "Professor George put a gyroscope into Boing-Boing so that he will always know which way is up or down. That's how he saved the trapeze artist when we went to the circus together."

"I remember, Danny," replied Amy. "But how does he hold on to the tree branches without falling?"

Daniel answered, "The last time Professor George fixed Boing-Boing he added new bionic claws to his paws. They're very sharp and the claws are almost as hard as diamonds. Professor George says they're made from a ceramic material called silicon carbide. Boing-Boing uses his new claws to hold tight onto the tree branch."

"Won't he scratch you with his claws when you hold him?" asked Amy.

"No," replied Daniel. "They're just like a real cat's and retract into his soft paws when he doesn't need them."

"That's really clever," said Amy.

"Professor George is always tinkering, adding useful things to Boing-Boing," said Daniel. "But every time I have to remind him not to reprogram the voice simulator to say 'Meow-Meow', instead of 'Boing-Boing'. He still thinks that was a bad mistake."

"I don't," said Amy. "I think saying his name instead of 'Meow-

Meow' when you press his nose is the
best thing about Boing-Boing. Look! He's
picked up your airplane with his teeth and is
climbing down backwards. How did he learn to
do that?"

"Professor George programmed Boing-Boing's
computer to follow my voice commands. I can teach
him to do just about anything," Daniel boasted.

Just then they heard a strange shout from the street.

"Dan! Dan! Are you home?"

Daniel's neighbor, Professor George, hurried towards
them. He looked a bit dishevelled – his cheeks were
flushed and his sweater out of place from rushing to find
his young neighbor.

"Yes, I'm here," answered Daniel. "What's the matter?"

"Hi Dan. Hi Amy," Professor George puffed between breaths. "Have I got news for you! Is Boing-Boing in good shape?"

"He's better than ever," Daniel quickly replied.

"Well, he will need to be," said Professor George, sitting down on the step and wiping his brow.

"I just received an urgent message from NASA. They have asked me to see if you and Boing-Boing can prevent a disaster."

"What has happened?" asked Daniel. "What could Boing-Boing and I do to help the space program?"

"It's the International Space Station!" answered Professor George. "They need you and Boing-Boing to help save it! Come inside and I will explain everything to you and your mother. We must hurry. There's not much time!"

chapter two

Professor George was not an ordinary professor. Like other professors he gave lectures and supervised students at the large university nearby, but he also directed a laboratory that did research on bionics and new types of robots. He had a workshop in his home next door to Daniel, where he built Boing-Boing. Since then Professor George and Daniel had become good friends and shared many adventures.

Daniel and his mom listened intently as Professor George told them his news;

"The International Space Station is in danger," he explained. "It might lose all communications with Earth. There is even a possibility that it could fall out of **orbit** and crash."

"Why?" asked Daniel, "What's gone wrong?"

"The problem is due to the Sun," answered Professor George. "Every eleven years there are huge storms on the Sun. These storms release enormous amounts of energy. The energy is in the form of particles that bombard the Earth. These powerful **solar flares** can do lots of damage, especially to **satellites** like the International Space Station."

"What sort of damage?" asked Daniel.

"Damage done to the electronics that control the International Space Station is one," answered Professor George. "Let me show you," he said, pulling from his briefcase a picture of a massive solar storm and its effects on Earth.

"You see Dan, during a solar storm the Sun emits a huge wave of billions and billions of high energy particles. The particles can blast into the computers and all the electronic controls on the International Space Station. The high energy X-rays travel at the speed of light and arrive at Earth within 8 minutes or so. A few days later, a powerful solar flare can even compress the magnetic field that surrounds the Earth. This is very important because the magnetic field around the Earth protects all living things, including us, from most of the high energy particles that come from outer space."

"That's awesome!" Daniel exclaimed.

"It is, Dan, but it is also very dangerous. There are more than 600 satellites in orbit around the Earth. Most of our communications today use one or more of these satellites. When you make a phone call or your mom uses her credit card the information goes to a central computer by way of a satellite. All of our weather is

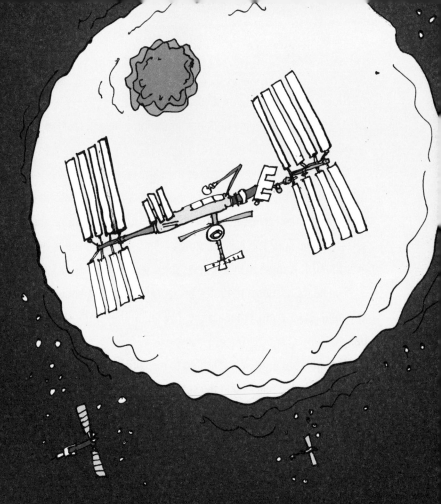

predicted by use of satellites. All of these are in danger of being damaged by the solar storms."

"How does NASA know that the International Space Station is in danger?" asked Daniel.

"There are early warning satellites in orbit looking for signs of solar storms, Dan," replied Professor George. "One of these warning satellites shows that in four days there is likely to be the biggest solar storm in a hundred years."

"How can the satellite predict such a large storm? The weatherman on TV is only right half of the time here in London," laughed Daniel.

"This photo was taken by one of the early warning satellites using an ultraviolet ray camera. It shows why a huge solar storm is likely," answered Professor George. "See the large dark spot on the surface of the Sun? It is called a **sunspot**. This sunspot is the largest ever found. It is more than ten times the size of Earth!"

"I've heard of sunspots, Professor George, but I don't know anything about them. What are they? What do they do?" asked Daniel.

"Sunspots are pretty complicated to explain, Dan. They are cooler and darker patches on the surface of the Sun caused by magnetic fields shaped like coiled tubes that rise from the interior of the star. The coiled tubes twist and turn as they rotate around the Sun heading towards its equator. These loops contain charged particles known as plasma."

"When the loops become disrupted by the surface pressure of the Sun they break and spew their contents of charged particles outwards. This causes a solar flare of radiation that reaches Earth in just a few minutes. A mass ejection called a coronal mass follows two to three days later. The massive wave of radiation slams into the Earth and compresses the **magnetic field** that protects all of us."

"Ouch," exclaimed Daniel. "You said this new sunspot is ten times bigger than Earth. That must mean it will make a huge solar flare. What is the largest flare we have been hit with, Professor George?"

"In November 2003 there was a solar eruption that measured at a magnitude of X-28, the largest recorded to date. Fortunately the Earth was spared much damage as the flare caught Earth at a glancing angle. But in 1989 a direct hit of a smaller flare knocked out the electricity supply of the Canadian state of Quebec. This huge, new sunspot is already producing powerful flares that have damaged the International Space Station."

"What will happen if there is a direct hit?" asked Daniel, fearfully.

"No one knows for sure," replied Professor George. "But unless the International Space Station can be turned from its present angle the effect will be disastrous. It could start to spin and fall out of its stable orbit and crash into the Earth."

"Why can't it be turned away from a direct hit?" asked Daniel.

"Normally it could be," answered Professor George. "But last week a large solar flare damaged the electronics of the large gyroscope that controls the position of the International Space Station. The huge wave of particles also damaged the solar panels that provide power to the Station. Now it's running on emergency levels of power until the solar panels can be fixed. That will have to wait until after this massive solar storm is over."

"You taught me about solar cells, Professor George," interrupted Daniel. "The solar panels on the International Space Station have the same type of solar cells that are inside Boing-Boing. They convert the sunlight transmitted through his fibre-optic fur into electricity that runs his computer."

"That's right, Dan. The International Space Station has the same type of power supply as your bionic cat."

"So, how can Boing-Boing help save the International Space Station?" asked Daniel. "Won't the solar flares damage him also?"

"I think we can protect Boing-Boing," replied Professor George. "I have done a quick calculation. It shows that if I put about one to two centimetres of lead and polyethylene shielding around Boing-Boing's computer it should be okay for one hour. That's about this much shielding," he said holding his fingers apart.

"But Professor George, lead is very heavy. How can Boing-Boing walk with all that extra weight? He has trouble now when his batteries get low," Daniel said, imagining Boing-Boing sluggishly shifting about with a new, lead-laden body.

"Dan, you forget that the International Space Station is in orbit 220 miles above us. They don't feel Earth's gravity because all objects in orbit are in free-fall. Boing-Boing's motors will run his legs just fine even with the lead and polyethylene around his belly. But we will have to make sure he has enough time to do the job since he will walk a little slower."

Though Daniel was relieved to hear this, he began to worry about each and every aspect of Boing-Boing's anatomy. "How about his bionic eyes?" he asked, "Will they be okay?"

"His bionic eyes could be a problem. I think I will need to add infrared transmitting glass lenses like he used in our trip to Egypt. The glass will be less sensitive to damage by the X-rays from the solar storm. I will also build him a polyethylene facemask. Polyethylene is very good at stopping several types of high energy particles."

"Boing-Boing's infrared eyes worked really well deep inside the pyramid in the dark," said Daniel. "Will they work out in space in the bright sunlight as well?"

"The International Space Station orbits the Earth at 17,500 miles per hour. That means it takes ninety minutes to go around the Earth. Half of the time it is in darkness, half in sunlight, or thereabouts. So, Dan, how long does it give Boing-Boing to do his mission in the **dark side of the orbit**?" asked Professor George.

"About forty-five minutes," answered Daniel quickly.

"That's right," replied Professor George. "I should be able to program his computer and adjust his bionic eyes for the length of the mission. But we have to find out if he will still follow your voice commands out in space."

Daniel gulped. "Am I going into space with Boing-Boing?"

"No. No. I'm sorry if I gave that impression," responded Professor George. "You will give your instructions from Earth at the Kennedy Space Center in Florida. Your commands will be beamed up to him. There is not enough time for you to be trained to go on the Space Shuttle – training can take years. There also isn't a space suit small enough for you," Professor George explained. He turned to Daniel's mother and quickly added, "Besides, it would be too dangerous. See, the reason NASA has asked if Boing-Boing can do this dangerous mission is because he is not alive. All living beings would be damaged by the high energy radiation."

"What can the radiation do?" asked Daniel.

"It can damage the **genes** in your cells," replied Professor George. "You know when you go to the dentist, Dan, or the doctor, and they take an **X-ray** of you, they always leave you alone in the room. It's because the energetic particles, like X-rays, can break the strands of **DNA** that make up your genes. Damaged genes can lead to cancer. That is why doctors and dentists limit the amount of radiation given to patients and how much they get exposed to it."

"What about the astronauts?" asked Daniel. "Aren't they in danger?"

"The living quarters in the International Space Station are shielded so the astronauts are relatively safe as long as they stay inside. If they go outside to install an emergency control **rocket** to change the orientation of the International Space Station or try to repair the solar panels they would probably not survive the strength of the expected solar flare."

"Won't their space suits protect them?" wondered Daniel.

"Not enough," answered Professor George. "Their space suits protect them by providing oxygen to breathe and control their temperature so they don't bake or freeze. But space suits cannot protect astronauts from large doses of high energy radiation."

"So my cat is the only chance the International Space Station has," Daniel said, amazed at the importance of the bundle of bionic fur sitting in his lap.

"That's about it," said Professor George . He had a serious look on his face. "If Boing-Boing can get up there fast enough and do the job, we think he can save the International Space Station."

Daniel looked to his mom for approval, hoping he could join in on another adventure with the Professor.

"Why don't you go pack a bag while I discuss some details with Professor George?" Daniel's mother said with a little worry on her face.

"All right!" yelled Daniel as he dashed from the room.

"And don't forget your toothbrush!" reminded his mother as he disappeared into his bedroom.

chapter three

As Daniel feverishly packed his bag, Professor George picked up Boing-Boing and dashed home next door. He quickly told Mrs. George about his latest adventure, and while she packed for him, he went down to the basement workshop. He opened up the panel in Boing-Boing's belly and connected wires from the small computer inside the cat to the computer terminal on his desk.

"Supie, check my calculations, will you?" he muttered as he logged on to the university supercomputer from his own computer. He typed in some commands and after a few minutes Supie had provided a list of the parts of the bionic cat that could be damaged by radiation from the solar flare.

A few more minutes and the computer screen showed how much lead and polyethylene shielding was needed to give Boing-Boing a 99.9% chance of surviving one hour of exposure to the predicted amount of radiation.

"So, my quick calculation was pretty close. You are going to need a lead box that is 0.85 centimetres thick around your computer, little fellow," he said to Boing-Boing. "Let's see if there is room inside."

Professor George selected some small sheets of lead from his store of metal, plastic and ceramic parts. He quickly molded the lead into a small box around the computer. Checking with the image on the computer screen he also wrapped lead around the critical junctions from the computer to Boing-Boing's other bionic parts to protect them from radiation. He then added infrared sensors to the bionic eyes. Finally, he wrapped all the electronic parts with polyethylene film and filled the spare space inside the bionic cat with polyethylene beads.

About a half-hour later he stretched, ate a few bites of the sandwich brought by Mrs. George and said, "Okay, little fellow, let's see if everything still works."

He pressed the ON button and the bionic cat's eyes glowed.

"Good," said Professor George. He then stroked the fibre-optic fur and the cat gave out a gentle "Puuurrrr."

"That's just right," responded Professor George. He then pressed on the cat's nose and it immediately responded with a loud "BOING-BOING".

Professor George laughed. "I will never forget my surprise when I first heard you say that the night I made you for Dan. Dan was so

sad. He couldn't have a cat because he was allergic to them. He was
so happy when he heard you say Boing-Boing. Just think of all the
adventures you've had since. I hope you survive this one!"

Professor George picked up the cat. "You're a lot heavier now,
aren't you?" he said as he turned on the program to make Boing-
Boing walk.

"One more change, Boing-Boing, and we are ready," muttered Professor George as he typed in another set of calculations to the computer.

A strange pattern of spirals appeared on the computer screen.

"That's it. Great!" he exclaimed. "I can adjust Boing-Boing's fibre-optic fur on one side to be a **Fresnel lens**. It is the same type of lens that is on most overhead projectors. That should make NASA's plan work."

Professor George carefully changed several rows of glass fibres until the pattern matched that shown on the computer.

"Let's see if you can focus this light, Boing-Boing," said Professor George as he shone a strong lamp on the side of the bionic cat.

"Great!" he exclaimed happily. "It makes a nice sharp beam of light. That is just what we will need.

Well, Boing-Boing, you seem to be working fine. All systems are Go. Now we will find out if you have the right stuff!"

chapter four

Daniel, Professor George and Boing-Boing were strapped into their seats in a supersonic military jet. It took off and quickly accelerated. Daniel focused on breathing as the jet's speed turned his stomach. Professor George had assured him the trip would only be five hours but Daniel now thought crossing the Atlantic Ocean should take even less time.

The professor saw Daniel's discomfort, and to focus him on their upcoming mission he said, "We are cleared to land at the Kennedy Space Center. We will come down on the same runway used by the Space Shuttle."

"I've seen the Shuttle land on the telly," Daniel replied. "It was so cool."

"It is hard to believe that it lands at twice the speed of a jet airliner, Dan. It lands with no power and almost always right in the middle of the runway," responded Professor George. "Your bionic cat should be quite safe getting to and from the International Space Station."

"You mean Boing-Boing's going on the Space Shuttle?" asked Daniel. "Wow! Will he be the first cat in space?"

"No, but he will be the first bionic cat," Professor George replied with a chuckle. "Do you know what the first animal in space was?"

"It was a dog, wasn't it?" replied Daniel as the professor nodded in agreement. "When was it launched?"

"Many years ago, in 1957. The Russian space program developed a very powerful booster rocket. They used it to put the first satellite into orbit, called Sputnik," said Professor George.

"I've heard of Sputnik," responded Daniel. "It was Sputnik that made President Kennedy want the United States to win the Space

Race and be the first to put a man on the moon."

"That's right, Dan. But several years before the Americans were able to send a man into orbit, the Russians had done so. They made sure the rocket and space capsule was safe by putting a dog named Laika into orbit. It was quite a triumph for them."

"Are the Americans and Russians still competing in the space race?"

"No," replied Professor George. "In fact the International Space Station is named just that because it is a product of international teamwork. Large parts of it are being built by the Russians. See, look at this drawing. All the parts coloured orange are being constructed and launched by the Russians. The parts in blue are being built by the Americans. Italy is building a module, it is coloured purple. Japan is making four modules, the entire continent of Europe is making a space lab for experiments, Brazil contributes one component and Canada has provided a bigger version of its famous robotic arm."

"Then Boing-Boing will be in good company," replied Daniel.

"Yes indeed, Dan!" the professor replied. "Many of the technical components built into your bionic cat are similar to those used in the International Space Station. He is in good shape to be the first Space Cat."

"When will Boing-Boing go up? Will he really be all right?" asked Daniel, realizing for the first time how much he was going to miss his cat. "How will I be able to give him instructions?"

"The Space Shuttle is already on the launch pad, ready to exit the atmosphere and connect to the International Space Station" replied Professor George. "There is a very tight launch window when the Shuttle can match the orbit of the International Space Station. So as soon as we land we will be rushed to the launch pad. The astronauts are already on board and the Shuttle is fuelled to take off. After it is gone I will give you the details of Boing-Boing's mission and the instructions you will need to give him. If all goes well, Boing-Boing will return safe and sound," the professor assured. Daniel could detect some worry in Professor George's voice. While Daniel was nervous about Boing-Boing's mission, he hoped that it would prove as successful as the bionic cat's previous adventures had in the past.

chapter five

The jet taxied to a stop, the door opened and Professor George gently shook Daniel's arm.

"Dan, wake up. It's show time."

Daniel yawned and looked out to see the bright Florida sunshine and palm trees.

"Are we there already?"

"Yes, Daniel," replied the person coming up the steps to the plane. "Hello, Professor George. Welcome to Kennedy Space Center. I am Dr Ann Andrews. All of us here at NASA are very pleased you could come on such short notice."

"Are you a doctor and an astronaut?" asked Daniel, in awe.

"Yes," replied Dr Andrews. "I am a Mission Specialist. I have two doctorates; one is in optical engineering and the second is in communication sciences. On this special emergency mission I am responsible for communications between you and your bionic cat.

May I please see him, Daniel?"

"Of course. Dr Andrews, meet Boing-Boing, the Bionic Cat," responded Daniel as he opened his travel bag and gently removed his cat. He switched the cat to ON and held him out to Dr Andrews.

"Stroke him and press his nose," suggested Daniel. The bionic cat's eyes lit up. He purred and then said, "Boing-Boing" as he looked up at the astronaut.

"He is marvellous, Daniel. I have heard about your adventures and the people you have saved. Working together I am sure that we can save the International Space Station," she said as they walked across the runway to a NASA van.

Doctor Andrews told Professor George and Daniel details of the mission as they raced to the launch pad.

"There's the Space Shuttle!" yelled Daniel as he saw it for the first time. He stood in wonder, staring up at the enormous spacecraft bound to what looked like three barrels, the largest in the centre. It towered over them.

"We go up into the Shuttle by this elevator," Dr Andrews said, as they quickly went higher and higher. "Now through this door, Daniel," she instructed.

"Wow!" he exclaimed as he looked around him at the astronaut's couches.

"Here's Boing-Boing's space suit and launch couch, Daniel," said Dr Andrews, showing them a special little chair and a small space suit made from Nomex, a flame resistant material. "This suit

will prevent any of Boing-Boing's fibre-optic fur from breaking off during launch and floating around when we are in space. We cannot take a chance of bits of glass getting in our eyes or in the equipment."

Dr Andrews turned to a man who had just appeared next to her, saying, "Daniel, I want you to meet Dr Alan Martin. He is the astronaut that will be in charge of Boing-Boing on board."

"Hello Daniel, very nice to meet you," said Dr Martin. "Do you mind if I call you Dan?"

"Of course not!" Daniel answered, still in awe at being inside the Space Shuttle.

"When I was your age," Dr Martin continued, "My hero was Dan Dare – it's because of him I became an astronaut! Now, let's see if the launch chair fits your bionic cat."

He carefully placed his bionic cat into the special chair and buckled Boing-Boing into place with a safety harness.

"It's perfect. How did you know his size?" asked Daniel.

"Before I left my workshop I downloaded Boing-Boing's design features and dimensions stored in Supie, the Super Computer, into the NASA computer here at the Kennedy Space Center," answered Professor George. "While we were flying, Dr Andrews and Dr Martin and the NASA machine shop here built Boing-Boing's launch seat. It will soften the forces of up to five-times gravity and prevent your bionic cat from being thrown about when the Space Shuttle accelerates."

"Wow!" exclaimed Daniel. "Five-times gravity. How do the astronauts survive?"

"Dan, acceleration at lift off is usually just three-times gravity, termed '3 G's,'" replied Dr Martin. "But, we designed into Boing-Boing's launch seat an extra margin of safety since we have never sent a bionic cat into space before."

"That's a good thing," said Daniel, looking around the crew compartment. "You definitely don't have room here for Professor George's workshop to fix Boing-Boing if something goes wrong."

"Here's something else special that we made for your bionic cat," said Dr Andrews showing Daniel a small pair of goggles.

"Are these sunglasses for Boing-Boing?" asked Daniel.

Dr Andrews confirmed that they were, adding, "They are very special sunglasses. They have electro-optical lenses developed to protect the eyes of U.S. Air Force pilots. The lenses are a special type of ceramic that can be either transparent to light or stop light completely. If there is a large flash of light from the Sun the lenses switch very fast to become dark. These goggles will protect Boing-Boing's bionic eyes while he is outside the International Space Station. The straps have small radio receivers and microphones which will transmit your voice to him."

"Excellent!" Daniel replied, feeling reassured as he adjusted the goggles on Boing-Boing.

"Daniel, we made something else special for your bionic cat. Can you see if it fits?" said Dr Andrews handing Daniel a small harness.

Daniel took Boing-Boing in his arms and fitted the straps around his cat.

"Snap the ends together underneath Boing-Boing," suggested Dr Andrews. "When the big red button is pushed it releases the harness. Try it, Daniel."

Daniel pressed on the button and Boing-Boing easily slipped out. "Why do you want Boing-Boing to wear this?" asked Daniel.

"The harness is how your bionic cat is going to carry a new steering rocket to the International Space Station," interjected the astronaut. "See, this is a model of the rocket that fits on the back of the harness, like so," Dr Andrews told Daniel while fitting it in place on Boing-Boing's back. "A small rocket will be put on him when we are at the International Space Station."

"Wow!" exclaimed Daniel, holding up his cat with the rocket on his back. "Boing-Boing, the Rocket Cat! That's cool! But, how will Boing-Boing get back?" asked Daniel with a worried frown on his face.

"That's what the red button is for, Daniel," replied Dr Andrews. "We know that you have taught Boing-Boing to recognize red objects and chase them. That's how you saved the little girl from the lion at the zoo and the trapeze artist. So, we thought you could instruct your bionic cat to press the red button with one of his paws and release the harness after he delivers the rocket to the right place. He can then go back inside the International Space Station and return to Earth on the Space Shuttle."

"Oh, I see," said Daniel, still with a worried look. "But won't the rocket just float away into space? How can it change the direction of the International Space Station?"

"Daniel, you're right. We admit that is the most risky part of the mission. The rocket has to be attached very firmly to the International Space Station. When it fires in one direction it will move the International Space Station in the opposite direction. Just like this," she said, showing Daniel a drawing.

"In order to work, the rocket must be attached to the International Space Station and be pointed in just the right direction. Our computers show the right location and the right direction. The rocket has to fire for just the right time. But the computers can't put the rocket there and start it firing. That's why we have turned to you and Boing-Boing. We need you to convert the calculations to action."

"Wow!" exclaimed Daniel. "How can Boing-Boing attach the

rocket to the International Space Station?"

"Dan, you will like this. We have worked out a plan for Boing-Boing to glue the rocket to the metal frame of the robotic arm of the International Space Station. The robotic arm is already locked into place. That way it won't make any difference if its control circuits are affected by the solar flares. You will give Boing-Boing commands to place the rocket at precisely the right location out at the end of the robotic arm. Look here at Boing-Boing's harness. See those stripes of blue colour?"

"Yes, what are they?" asked Daniel.

"Each stripe is a special type of glue that becomes very hard when it is exposed to ultraviolet light. It is like the material dentists use to fill cavities in your teeth," answered Dr Andrews. "During the dark side of the orbit we plan to have you direct Boing-Boing to the right location and unfasten the harness and the rocket. Then we want you to have your bionic cat move a few steps away. When

the Sun comes up its light will be focused by Boing-Boing's fibre-optic lens onto the harness to melt and activate the stripes of glue. They will fix the harness and the rocket to the aluminum frame."

"Is that why Boing-Boing's fur has those funny patterns on one side, Professor George?" asked Daniel.

"Yes," replied Professor George. "They are a special type of lens called a Fresnel lens."

"Boing-Boing, you are even more special, aren't you?" Daniel asked his cat while stroking his nose.

"BOING-BOING!" replied his bionic cat as everyone laughed.

"Sorry, time for you to leave. Thirty minutes to launch. Time for the countdown," Dr Martin said to Dr Andrews, Daniel and Professor George.

"Okay, but first, Daniel, every astronaut is allowed to take one personal item with them on a mission. Is there anything that Boing-Boing would like to take?" Dr Martin asked.

"That's neat!" responded Daniel. "Yes. Can Boing-Boing take along his favorite red ball? He loves to chase it when I ask him. It would be fun to see if he can catch it while floating in free fall."

"Good idea, Daniel," replied Dr Martin. "You can use the red ball to practice Boing-Boing's commands before he goes EVA."

"What's EVA?" asked Daniel.

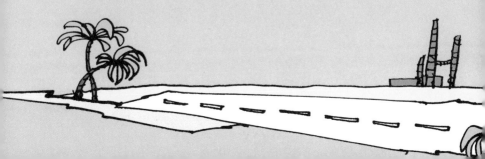

"EVA stands for Extra-Vehicular Activity, Dan. It is space jargon for a space walk," replied Dr Martin.

"Time to go, Daniel," said Dr Andrews as a warning gong sounded. "Say good-bye to Boing-Boing. He should be back in a few days, if all goes well."

"Bye-bye, Boing-Boing," said Daniel with a lump in his throat as he gently stroked his bionic cat. "I will miss you."

His cat looked up at him and replied, "BOING-BOING, BOING-BOING."

Chapter Six

Daniel, Professor George and Dr Andrews joined the astronauts' families at the press building two miles from the Space Shuttle launch pad.

"Dan, it won't be long now," said Professor George. "See the **vapor** coming from the Shuttle's main engine? It is almost ready for ignition. Listen to the countdown."

Over the loudspeaker came the exciting countdown:

10-9-8-7-6

5-4-3-2-1

IGNITION!

A huge plume of flame came from the Shuttle's main engine and the booster rockets. An enormous cloud of vapor erupted from the pit of water protecting the launch pad. Slowly, ever so slowly the massive space vehicle lifted from the pad.

BOOOOOOOOOOMMMMM!!!

Sound rocked the press gallery and everyone in it.

"Did you feel that, Professor George?" Daniel asked, shocked that the sound from the shuttle's powerful engines almost knocked him over. "I sure did, Daniel," replied Professor George. "Look! It really accelerates now that it is off the ground."

Faster and faster, the Space Shuttle moved upwards. The flames from the engines were so bright Daniel could hardly look at it.

"Look! Look, Professor George!" shouted Daniel. "It's turning over! It's upside down!"

"The Shuttle changes its orientation after it reaches a certain height. Now watch," responded Professor George as Daniel's eyes grew wider at the sight of the enormous craft disassembling in mid-air. The professor explained, "The booster rockets are separating from the Shuttle. That happens 2 minutes and 8 seconds after launch."

"Incredible..." Daniel muttered, his eyes following the shuttle rising up and up.

"Yes," replied Dr Andrews. "They are solid fuel rockets. They have done their job and now they will be recovered by a ship and refuelled, to be used again. They have been used over and over and are one of the reasons that the Space Shuttle has been successful for many years. It has taken more than ten Shuttle missions to build the International Space Station. It is the size of three football fields. You can see it with binoculars when it passes overhead."

"Can you still see the Shuttle?" Daniel asked as he became anxious at the thought of his cat so high in the sky.

"No," replied Professor George. "It is five minutes after lift-off and the Shuttle is already half-way to Africa. It is travelling now at about 10,000 miles per hour. See, look here," he said, showing Daniel a drawing, "In a half hour the Shuttle will be in orbit."

"What happens then?" asked Daniel.

Professor George pointed to the drawing. He said, "Once in orbit, the Shuttle will be chasing the International Space Station, which is in a higher orbit, about 220 miles up."

"How will the Shuttle catch it?" asked Daniel, puzzled.

"The Shuttle will continue to fire its engines until it reaches enough velocity to intercept the International Space Station. There are only a few launch windows every month when this is possible. That is why you had to get here so quickly," responded Dr Andrews.

"I wonder what Boing-Boing is doing now?" asked Daniel.

"I will get a report for you, Daniel," replied Dr Andrews.

"Dr Martin, can you hear me?" she inquired into a microphone.

"All clear!" he replied. "We are now in orbit. All systems are operating fine. We should reach the International Space Station on schedule."

"Alan, here's Daniel. Do you have time to speak to him?"

"Sure. Hi, Dan. Did you enjoy the launch?" asked Dr Martin.

"It was fantastic!" replied Daniel. "I have never seen or felt anything like it. How's Boing-Boing? Did he survive the launch? Is he okay?"

"I have just finished checking him out, Dan. I'll let you see for yourself. Check the video," Dr Martin replied.

"Flip that switch, Daniel," instructed Dr Andrews. "It activates the video camera in the crew compartment."

Daniel flipped the switch and the TV screen lit up. Immediately he saw an image of the inside of the Shuttle cabin where Dr Martin unstrapped the little orange bundle from the seat next to him.

Once unstrapped, Boing-Boing began to float about the cabin as Danny watched on the screen. "That's incredible! Look at him go!" shouted Daniel.

"Ann, can you hear me? Can you see Boing-Boing clearly?" Dr Martin called down.

"Everything is just fine, Alan," replied Dr Andrews.

"Let's check out Boing-Boing's systems and make sure everything is working before you arrive at the Space Station."

"Right," replied Dr Martin. "What do you want me to check first?"

"Daniel, find out if he still responds to your voice," requested Dr Andrews.

"Okay," replied Daniel." But he needs to be turned on first before he can hear my commands."

"I've got him, Dan," said Dr Martin as he gently caught Boing-Boing in the middle of a somersault. He turned Boing-Boing over, opened the front of the suit and pushed the ON button.

Boing-Boing's eyes lit up and shone through the goggles.

"That's great!" said Daniel. "He is okay so far. BOING-BOING, TURN YOUR HEAD LEFT," commanded Daniel.

Boing-Boing's head turned towards the video camera.

Daniel, Professor George and Dr Andrews could see him almost face to face.

"Great!" shouted Daniel. "He can still follow my commands."

"Dan, see if Boing-Boing's new video cameras are working," said Professor George. "I added a very small one to each eye before we left. We need to see if they work with his goggles on."

"How do I do that?" asked Daniel.

"The voice activated computer command, Daniel, is 'Boing-Boing, video on,'" replied Professor George.

"Okay," said Daniel. "I will give it a go. BOING-BOING, VIDEO ON."

An image of the inside of the Space Shuttle mid-deck appeared on the screen in front of Daniel, Professor George and Dr Andrews.

"BOING-BOING, MOVE RIGHT," commanded Daniel.

Slowly his bionic cat began to change direction as he floated in the cabin. The small video cameras showed the view of the cabin slowly changing until Dr Martin came into view. He had Boing-Boing's red ball in his hand.

"BOING-BOING, FETCH THE RED BALL," commanded Daniel.

Boing-Boing pushed gently off a wall with his legs to get some momentum. He began slowly to move towards the ball, his paws moving back and forth in the air to change direction. Dr Martin gently tossed the ball upwards. It floated up a few inches and floated in space.

Boing-Boing floated towards the ball and in a few moments caught up with it. He reached out with his front paws and extended his new bionic claws. They gently grasped the ball.

"BOING-BOING, FIND DR MARTIN. TAKE THE RED BALL TO DR MARTIN," commanded Daniel.

Slowly the bionic cat moved his head. His bionic eyes found the astronaut. The small video cameras in his eyes showed him push off another wall and slowly move toward Dr Martin. Boing-Boing reached out and gave him the ball.

"Yes! Well done, Boing-Boing!" exclaimed Daniel, pumping his fist in the air as everyone cheered.

The news commentators broadcasting the event said they could hardly believe their eyes. Millions of people watching throughout the world cheered for the new bionic hero.

"This proves the mission of saving the International Space Station has a very good chance of success," proclaimed the NASA spokesman in a news program interview.

"It sure does!" said Daniel and Professor George at the same time with huge grins on their faces.

Chapter Seven

After a meal and some much needed sleep, Dr Andrews gently woke Daniel and Professor George.

"Sorry to disturb you. The Shuttle has reached the International Space Station and is docking now. It won't be long before Boing-Boing will be going on his EVA."

Daniel gulped. So far everything had been a great adventure. There was no time to think of danger. He now realized that maybe something could go wrong. He remembered how sad he was when he left Boing-Boing behind in the Natural History Museum. He also remembered how relieved he was when he got him back after Boing-Boing helped catch the jewel thief.

It finally hit him. Boing-Boing could be lost in space.

Boing-Boing could be gone forever.

As Daniel gulped, Dr Martin's voice boomed out of the speaker. He was in his space suit.

"Dan, can you see your rocket cat?"

Daniel looked up. There was Boing-Boing with a real rocket on his harness.

"Cool!" said Daniel. "It's ... it's so big," He continued, astonished that his small house-pet would soon be transporting an enormously powerful rocket, alone. He was reassured by Professor George's explanation that Boing-Boing wouldn't feel the Earth's gravity that high up.

"Yes," replied the astronaut. "It is a solid fuel rocket that has a short burst with a lot of thrust. It should rotate the International Space Station to just the right angle to protect it from the solar flare. We go into dark side orbit in ten minutes. That's enough time for your rocket cat to get through the air lock. I'll take him through the inner door. I will come back inside. Then it will be up to you to give him directions when the outer door comes open. Use his eyes and video camera like your own eyes. Good luck, a lot depends on you and your cat."

Daniel gulped again and wiped some drops of sweat from his forehead. "As if I needed reminding," he thought to himself.

"Okay, Dr Martin," he answered. "You can count on us."

Dr Martin took Boing-Boing through the airlock and plugged the bionic cat's fibre-optics communication cable into a connector panel.

"Daniel, use the communications cable attached to Boing-Boing the same way you did when you directed him inside the pyramid," suggested Professor George.

"Okay, we're ready," replied Daniel.

Dr Martin, now safely back inside the crew compartment of the International Space Station, called to Daniel. "I can see your rocket cat on the monitor. The outer door is open. Go ahead and direct him outside and along the support beam. Take your time."

"BOING-BOING, MOVE FORWARD," commanded Daniel.

The bionic cat followed Daniel's directions and moved through the airlock.

Dan stared at the screen, overwhelmed with what his cat was seeing, "I can see stars! Billions and billions of stars!"

The video screen was filled with stars. Everywhere Boing-Boing turned his head were stars and more stars.

"They are very bright, aren't they?" Daniel said to Professor George.

"Yes, Daniel. Without Earth's atmosphere to spread out their light the stars shine much brighter than you can see down here. That's the reason for putting observatories like the Hubble Space Telescope in orbit."

Daniel proceeded to direct Boing-Boing along the beam towards the robotic arm where the rocket was needed.

"Professor George," called out Daniel. "His new bionic claws work really well. He isn't slipping at all."

"That's great, Dan," replied Professor George. "The sharp claws give just the right amount of grip on two feet so he can move forward with the other two even without the Earth's gravity."

A camera showed Boing-Boing's progress. "He's about halfway," said Daniel.

Dr Martin was keeping track of the time. It was critical that the rocket be at the right location as the Sun came up in order to glue it in place.

"Daniel. We are two minutes into our safety margin. Can you hurry him up a little?" asked Dr Martin.

"All right," agreed Daniel.

"BOING-BOING. GO A LITTLE FASTER," ordered Daniel.

His bionic cat immediately started to move his feet more quickly but still carefully as he climbed up the robotic arm.

"All the games Boing-Boing and I play are paying off now," said Daniel. "He remembers all his tricks."

"Great," said Dr Martin a few minutes later. "Your cat has reached exactly the right spot on the arm where the computer calculations show the rocket is needed."

"BOING-BOING, STOP," commanded Daniel, happy to see his space cat come to a halt through the video transmission eyes.

chapter eight

Dr Martin quickly checked the time and Boing-Boing's position against the computer image.

"Five minutes before sunrise, Dan," he called down. "He's a little out of position. Move him 7 degrees to the left."

"BOING-BOING, TURN LEFT, 1 degree, 2, 3, 4, 5, 6, 7 degrees. STOP!"

"How's that?" he asked Dr Martin.

"Perfect, Dan. Spot on. Rocket-cat's image matches the computer image perfectly. One minute to go. Watch for the sunrise and see if the lens on Boing-Boing's fur works the way Professor George has designed it to work."

Just then, an incredibly beautiful image appeared on the video screen. The Sun burst into view; it was an intense beam of light against the deep blackness of space. The powerful rays of the sunlight reflected from the fibre-optic fur of Boing-Boing. It looked like the bionic cat was glowing with the brilliance of millions of diamonds. Incredible patterns of light refracted into hundreds of rainbows shimmered from the fur.

Best of all, the special lens built into Boing-Boing's fur focused the Sun's rays into an intense beam of light. There was light of every wavelength, visible light, ultraviolet light and infrared light. The bright infrared light created a burst of heat that melted in an instant the special threads of glue woven into Boing-Boing's harness. The ultraviolet light just as quickly transformed the molten glue into a rock hard bond.

Daniel saw the flash of light that froze Boing-Boing to the support beam.

"It worked!" he yelled. "It worked!"

Boing-Boing was stuck fast to the beam. He could not move a bit. The rocket was ready to go.

"Great!" exclaimed Dr Martin.

"Well done, Daniel. Congratulations!" said Dr Andrews and Professor George.

"Now, you need to get rocket cat out of there, Dan," called Dr Martin. "Can you get him out of his harness?"

"I sure can!" replied Daniel, eager to see his cat safely back inside the International Space Station.

"BOING-BOING, PRESS THE RED BUTTON," commanded Daniel.

His bionic cat lifted up one of his front legs and pressed it against the big red button to release his harness.

Nothing happened.

"Oh no!" exclaimed Daniel. "Something must be wrong!"

"Try again," called out Dr Martin. "It seems to be stuck."

"BOING-BOING, PRESS THE RED BUTTON," called out Daniel much louder.

Still nothing.

Daniel began to get cold all over. "Is Boing-Boing going to be trapped on the Space Station forever?" he was thinking. "How could his cat survive the flames when the rocket blasted away? Would they sacrifice Boing-Boing to save the International Space Station?"

Daniel couldn't bear the thought. But what could he do?

Daniel quickly muttered to himself, "I must not panic. I must think. What were all the tricks that Amy and I thought up for Boing-Boing to do? Would one of them help?"

Chapter nine

Refusing to let panic overtake him, Daniel calmed down. He had an idea. Maybe the harness had got twisted a little when Boing-Boing had speeded up crawling along the arm. Perhaps what was needed was to loosen the straps a little. Maybe Boing-Boing could jiggle the straps loose.

How could he get him to do that?

A funny memory flashed into his mind.

It was one of Boing-Boing's favorite tricks he did to amuse his friends.

"I've got it!" shouted Daniel.

"BOING-BOING, DANCE!"

Boing-Boing's computer could not decide what to do, it didn't understand the command.

So Boing-Boing did the next best thing – he did nothing.

Daniel was startled. Boing-Boing had never refused a command before. He did not know what was wrong. Daniel thought, "This has to work, there must be a way."

Just then, an announcement came over the loud speaker.

"EMERGENCY! EMERGENCY! The solar warning satellite has detected an enormous solar flare is about to occur. It is projected to be three times larger than ever recorded before. This will be the solar storm of the century. We must get the International Space Station turned before it hits. We have 8 minutes before the advance wave of high energy X-rays hit. We have 15 to 20 minutes until the leading edge of a massive wave of energy hits. EMERGENCY! EMERGENCY!"

The shock of the emergency warning hit Daniel at just the right moment. It tripped his memory.

"I've got it!" he shouted.

"BOING-BOING, DANCE FOR JAMES AND ROBERT," commanded Daniel. In his rush, he had forgotten the complete command to Boing-Boing's computer. "No wonder Boing-Boing didn't know what to do," thought Daniel.

This time his bionic cat's computer recognized the command. There was no uncertainty as to what was wanted.

Boing-Boing immediately began to move his legs and head to the recorded beat of James, Robert and Daniel's clapping and singing.

He jiggled and he wiggled and he jigged and he jogged. His harness started to slip and slide on his fibre-optic fur.

Everyone laughed at the sight, even the astronauts. Back home on Earth all the TV stations were covering the crisis. There was an instant craze. All the kids across the world started to do what was quickly named The Boing-Boing Boogie.

"That should do it!" thought Daniel.

"BOING-BOING, STOP," ordered Daniel. His bionic cat immediately stopped the dance.

"FIVE MINUTES BEFORE THE FIRST WAVE HITS!" boomed out of the emergency speaker.

Daniel did not panic. He stayed cool.

"BOING-BOING, PRESS THE RED BUTTON," shouted Daniel down the communications cable.

Boing-Boing lifted one of his paws. He reached up and pressed hard on the big red button.

SNAP! The harness parted. He was free at last.

"YEAH! Three cheers for Boing-Boing!" cried everyone in the control room.

"Three cheers for Boing-Boing!" was heard all over the world, as the TV audiences cried out in relief.

"BOING-BOING, TURN AROUND," commanded Daniel. His cat obeyed and he started back down the long beam of the robotic arm.

"TWO MINUTES UNTIL THE FIRST WAVE HITS!" came out of the emergency speaker.

"BOING-BOING, FASTER, FASTER," yelled Daniel.

"ONE MINUTE!" warned the emergency speaker.

"BOING-BOING, FASTER, FASTER!" yelled Daniel who couldn't stand to see his much loved bionic cat still in danger.

Boing-Boing was close. He was only six meters away, only 30 steps from safety.

But then disaster struck.

The first wave of solar particles hit with a massive jolt of energy. They slammed into the outer solar panels, shorting out electric controls. They slammed into the robotic arm holding Boing-Boing's harness and the rocket attached to the arm. The energy of the particles was instantly absorbed by the metal. A wave of **electrons** and pulse of heat travelled in a flash up the arm and hit the rocket. The igniters went off and the rocket fired.

Professor George, Dr Andrews and Daniel watched on the screen as a massive blast turned the International Space Station. The rocket pushing on the anchored robotic arm rotated the living quarters of the International Space Station just enough. The extra shielding would protect the astronauts and the computers and controls.

When the rocket went off it went with a boom. No one watching heard the boom. You don't hear booms in space because there is no air to carry the sound waves.

But you can feel the boom. You can feel the boom especially if you are a small bionic cat. You can feel the boom especially if you are stepping quickly along the metal arm connected to the rocket.

"OH NO!" yelled Daniel. "OH NO! Look what's happened to Boing-Boing. He's floating off into space!"

Everyone looked and gasped. Daniel could do nothing but watch Boing-Boing helplessly float into the blackness of space. The rocket blast had caught him in mid stride. Three paws with their bionic claws were retracted. The claws of one paw were not enough to keep him on the beam. He was thrown off the beam.

"TEN MINUTES UNTIL THE BIG WAVE HITS!" blared the emergency speaker.

Daniel was close to panic. It looked like he was going to lose Boing-Boing after all.

"Daniel, look!" cried out Dr Andrews. "Boing-Boing is still attached to his communication cable. You can still give him commands."

"I know," said Daniel fearfully. "But what commands can I give him? He's floating away from the International Space Station. He will float away until he is at the end of the cable."

"You're right, Daniel," replied Dr Andrews. "The cable has many twists in it. If the twists are pulled tight it will break the glass fibres in the cable. We must find another way to pull him. Do you have any ideas? Making him dance worked, can you think of something else as clever?"

"SEVEN MINUTES UNTIL THE BIG WAVE HITS!" boomed the emergency speaker.

"We have to do something fast!" said Professor George.

"I know. I know!" replied Daniel, trying not to panic.

"I've got it!" he yelled, remembering another game he played with Boing-Boing and his friends.

"Dr Martin, can you hear me?" he asked.

"Yes, Daniel. Do you have an idea?" replied the astronaut.

"I do. Do you still have Boing-Boing's red ball?" asked Daniel.

"Yes, what good is it?" replied Dr Martin. "Your cat can't chase it in space."

"Oh yes he can!" cried out Daniel. "Have someone tie loops of cord around the ball while you put on your space suit. Then go into the airlock, open it a little and throw the ball out close enough for Boing-Boing to get it. Boing-Boing and I will do the rest."

"Sounds like a plan," replied Dr Martin, already putting on his space gear.

"FIVE MINUTES UNTIL THE BIG WAVE HITS!" proclaimed the emergency speaker.

"We don't have much time, Daniel," said Professor George. "Boing-Boing's shielding can't protect him from a solar flare this intense. It will destroy his computer for sure, then you won't be able to give him any commands to save him."

"FOUR MINUTES UNTIL THE BIG WAVE HITS!"

"I'm ready, Dan," said Dr Martin coming into view on the video screen with his space suit on. "I set a record getting into this thing. It usually takes an hour to check everything out but I kept most of it on from my first trip to the airlock. What do you want me to do now, Dan? You're the man!"

"Dr Martin, can you open the outer airlock just a little and throw the ball softly towards Boing-Boing as I give him a command?" asked Daniel.

"Okay," replied Dr Martin.

The red ball attached to a strong line slowly floated towards Boing-Boing who was dangerously close to the end of his cable.

"BOING-BOING, FETCH THE RED BALL," commanded Daniel.

This was a welcome command to Boing-Boing. He had played 'fetch the ball' for hours with Daniel, James and Robert in the back garden. It was really good fun to see how quickly he could get to it.

The red ball was ever so close. Just one paw length away.

Daniel watched as Boing-Boing struggled to propel himself forward without any friction. The cat stretched and stretched, pushing his entire body as far forward as possible. But the new environment was too unfamiliar and no matter what he did, Boing-Boing couldn't move forward. Then, due to Professor George's clever trial and error program, Boing-Boing tried pulling against the resistance of the communications cable, his one link back to the station.

"He's got it!" yelled Dr Martin. "The cat's got it!"

"Yeah!" yelled Daniel watching Boing-Boing inch his way back to the station.

"Three cheers for Boing-Boing!" yelled Professor George and Dr Andrews.

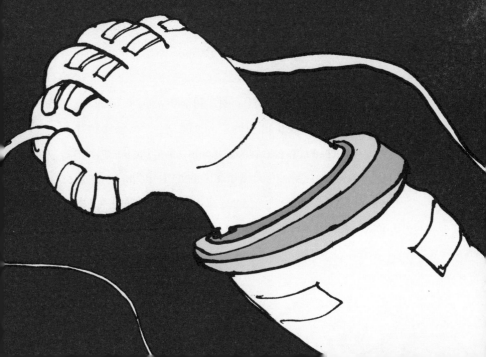

"Another marvellous rescue from outer space!" announced the TV commentator to viewers all over the world.

Boing-Boing's eyes showed the International Space Station getting closer and closer. The cameras on board showed the bionic cat being carefully reeled in by Dr Martin, pulling on the cord tied to the red ball.

"ONE MINUTE UNTIL THE BIG WAVE HITS!"

Boing-Boing moved closer, closer, closer. Finally, Boing-Boing was inside the International Space Station.

"TEN SECONDS UNTIL THE BIG WAVE HITS!"

The outer airlock door slammed shut.

"EIGHT SECONDS!"

The inner door slammed shut.

"SEVEN SECONDS!"

"He's safe!" shouted Daniel.

Daniel, Professor George, Dr Martin, Dr Andrews and the whole world laughed in great relief.

Professor George, turning to Daniel, said with a laugh, "Well done, Daniel. Look at the digital clock. Only 007 seconds to spare. I guess everyone can now call your cat 'Boing-Boing the Bond Cat'?"

Daniel, looking back with a big grin replied, "Or Boing-Boing the James Bond Cat??? Whatever people call him I guess we all agree that under pressure Boing-Boing is a really cool cat!"

The end

Maybe Yes and Maybe No.
Only Time Will Tell.

Solar Storms

Solar storms can make radios and other electronic devices stop working. They can also cause satellites like the International Space Station to fall out of orbit by heating and expanding the upper atmosphere, which makes the satellites slow down. Solar storms happen after shockwaves of radiation particles from the Sun reach the Earth's atmosphere. The shockwaves are caused by high energy events on the sun like solar flares. These flares are large eruptions that often make it look like the Sun is whipping a tail of fire.

To learn more about solar storms visit our website.

What happens in space...

Every 11 years the Sun's activity rises to a violent peak. During this interval, called the solar maximum, the Sun showers the Earth with highly energetic particles and radiation.

48 to 96 hours

The Earth's magnetic field is shaken by masses of solar particles, endangering power grids.

Great ball of fire

An immense, twisting solar eruption, filled with ionized helium gases as hot as 60,000 degrees C, escapes from the Sun (as seen by SOHO satellite in extreme UV light).

8 minutes

Ultraviolet and X-rays, travelling at the speed of light can black out radio transmissions.

30 minutes

Highly energetic, charged particles arrive, threatening satellites and high flying jets.

solar storm of the century

...and what could happen near Earth.

SATELLITES
Energetic particles can fry the electronics of the 600 satellites circling the Earth, rendering them useless.

AEROPLANES
A blast from the Sun can shower jet passengers with as much radiation as they would get from several chest X-rays.

POWER GRIDS
The magnetic field, jolted by blasts from the Sun, causes electrical surges in power lines, blowing out transformers.

PIPELINES
Heavy current induces oil and gas lines to leak at grounded points, accelerating corrosion and weakening the metal.

SPACECRAFT
Intense solar radiation can heat and expand the Earth's atmosphere, creating extra drag on satellites and decaying their orbits.

RADIO TRANSMISSIONS
Solar outpouring can degrade communications between ground controllers and satellites.

Earth

Compressed magnetosphere

Usual position of magnetosphere

The MAGNETOSPHERE, the region in space occupied by the Earth's magnetic field, usually extends outwards for 40,000 miles (64,000 km) on the Sun ward side, but fierce solar storms can compress the magnetosphere to only 26,000 miles (42,000 km) exposing high-orbiting satellites to the solar system.

Radiation

Radiation is energy that travels from one place to another as light or sub-atomic particles. Radiation comes in many forms depending on how much energy it carries. Visible light and radio frequencies are both types of radiation with low energy waves. Ultraviolet light and X-rays are examples of high energy radiation. Sub-atomic particle radiation includes things like cosmic rays from space and neutrons emitted by radioactive elements.

Ultraviolet Light

Ultraviolet light (or UV light) is a high energy radiation
that comes from the sun. Though it is a type of light it
is invisible to people. UV light is very dangerous and
the Earth's atmosphere blocks almost all UV radiation,
but the little bits that get through are still enough to
cause sunburn. During a short spacewalk, an astronaut
can take in as much radiation as they would in a year
on Earth. A large burst of ultraviolet radiation during
a solar storm can damage less powerful radio and
electronic equipment, and also move a satellite, maybe
making it fall to Earth. Ultraviolet light has more energy
than regular light, so new types of solar cells being
invented today will be able to get more electricity from
sunlight than traditional solar cells.

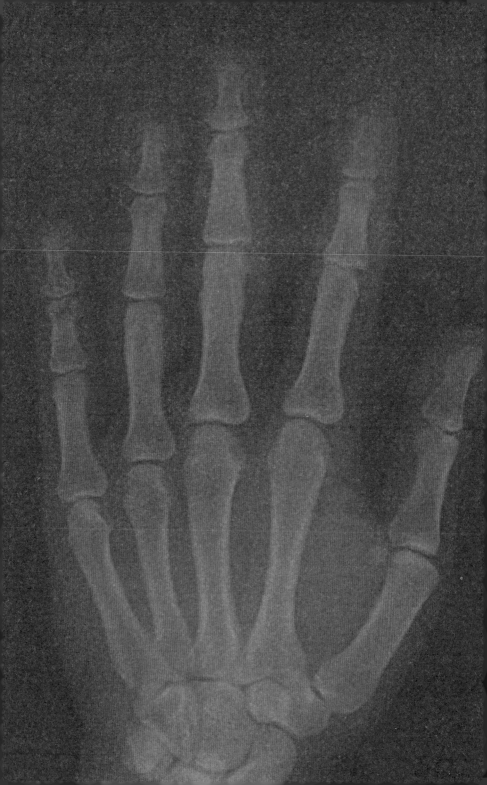

X-rays

X-rays (or X-radiation) are another type of radiation which is commonly used to take photographs of bones because the waves are strong enough to pass through some materials like skin. Being more powerful than ultraviolet light, X-rays are still dangerous enough to harm people, and you should always wear protection when taking an X-ray.

International Space Station

The International Space Station (or ISS) is a satellite
many countries started building in Earth's orbit in
1998. When the space station is completed in 2011 it
will be the largest satellite ever put into Earth's orbit.
Even though it is the world's largest space station,
only six people can live in it at one time. Astronauts
and scientists from all over the world go to the space
station to do experiments about living in space and to
study the stars. The International Space Station is also
used to test new equipment that can be used on long
missions to the Moon and Mars. In 2002 Canada added
a large robotic arm to the International Space Station.

Robotic Arm

The robotic arm on the International Space Station measures 17.6 meters (57.7 ft) and weighs 1,800 kilograms (3,970 lbs). The arm is used to easily put new pieces of the space station into place, and to move supplies to where they are needed. The robotic arm also helps astronauts because they attach their spacesuits to it so they can safely move around the outside of the International Space Station when making repairs.

Boing-Boing Space Station Glossary

DNA: A large double helix molecule that carries genetic information (instructions for making and operating a living thing). DNA determines your appearance, such as eye and hair color. DNA is copied and inherited across generations, which is why patterns in appearance occur from parents to children.

Dark side of the orbit: As a satellite orbits the Earth it may pass through the Earth's shadow. The part of the orbit in darkness is called the dark side.

Electron: A tiny particle with a negative electric charge. Electrons can orbit the nucleus of an atom or move on their own.

Fresnel lens: A thin flat optical lens that can concentrate light to a very bright spot. Used in lighthouses, spotlights, and solar energy.

Gene: Made of strands of DNA that code replication of molecular structures, for example proteins, that are essential to life.

Magnetic field: Surrounds magnetic objects and electrical currents. It is measured by its direction and strength. It is detected by the effect it has on magnetic objects and electrical charges. The Earth has its own magnetic field which protects it from the Sun's radiation by deflecting charged particles.

NOMEX®: A fabric used in space and firefighter's suits that has been designed with excellent thermal, chemical and radiation resistance.

Orbit: The path an object takes when it revolves around another object, such as the paths satellites, like the International Space Station or the moon, take revolving around Earth.

Polyethylene: The most widely used type of plastic, commonly used to make grocery bags.

Rocket: An engine that propels itself by burning fuel to produce exhaust gases. The engine pushes the gases backwards and the equal and opposite force of the gases push the engine forward.

Satellite: An object that orbits around a planet. An example of a natural satellite is the Moon, which orbits around the Earth. An artificial satellite, such as the International Space Station, has been placed in space by humans.

Silicon carbide (SiC): It is very rare on Earth, unless man-made, but remarkably common in space. This 'stardust' has been found in many meterorites, and it is prized for its hardness and sharpness.

Solar flares: A large explosion in the Sun's atmosphere that creates a shockwave of high energy particles. Solar flares often look like flaming tails whipping off of the Sun.

Sunspot: An area on the Sun that looks darker because it is cooler than the rest of the Sun. These 'cool' spots still reach about 3,700° C or 6,700° F!

Ultraviolet (UV) camera: A camera that can take images of ultraviolet light, which humans cannot see.

Vapor: The gas phase of a substance that can also exist in liquid and solid forms. The steam rising from a hot cup of tea would be an example of vaporized water. When water vapor condenses it becomes liquid water, and when it freezes it becomes a solid, ice.

Additional Resources

The World Wide Web is a great place to find out more about space, science and engineering. The following links all have some fun stuff and can be found on **www.canofwormsenterprises.co.uk/boingboing** to save you typing them in.

To see what Boing-Boing is up to visit: www.boing-boingfoundation.com

http://www.nasa.gov
The National Aeronautics and Space Administration's homepage.

http://science.nasa.gov/kids
Fun NASA website with links to science facts, games and quizzes.

http://solarsystem.nasa.gov/kids
Information about the solar system, including 'build your own space fleet'.

http://www.esa.int/esaKIDSen
European Space Agency's site, with facts about the universe & life as an astronaut.

http://www.esa.int/SPECIALS/Track_ESA_missions
Lets you track satellites, including the International Space Station!

http://www.nasa.gov/audience/forkids/kidsclub/flash
Interactive site with games, information on missions, & great pictures.

http://www.kidsastronomy.com
Facts about the solar system, space exploration, stars, the universe and more.

http://www.discoverengineering.org
Find out about engineering as a profession, plus activities, videos & games.

http://www.engineeringinteract.org
Games for teaching science with animated interactive explanations.

http://i.usatoday.net/tech/graphics/iss_timeline/flash.htm
Animation showing how the International Space Station is put together.

http://www.miravi.eo.esa.int/en
See the earth from above with satellite images.

http://www.spaceweather.com
News and facts about the conditions on the sun, asteroids, etc.

About the author

In addition to being the creator of Boing-Boing, Professor Larry Hench is a world-renowned scientist and engineer. He is credited with the discovery in the late 1960s of Bioglass®, the first man-made material to bond to living tissues – helping millions of people world-wide; and he continues to discover new applications in biomaterials for this amazing material.

His children's books extend his love of teaching, science and engineering to a new generation. All the technology built into the stories is scientifically valid and could be achieved using practical engineering materials and technology. The inspiration for these books comes from his nine grandchildren.

A graduate of The Ohio State University, Professor Hench is a Fellow of the American Ceramic Society and many other professional societies – Hench's numerous achievements, honors, scholarly writings and patents, over his long career, span several fields; including radiation damage, nuclear waste solidification, advanced optical materials, origins of life, ethics, technology transfer and entrepreneurship, bioceramics science and clinical applications and most recently, energy storage and conservation technologies.

Larry L. Hench, Ph.D., is currently Adjunct Graduate Research Professor at the University of Florida, Gainesville, Florida, Professor and Director of Special Projects at the University of Central Florida, Orlando, Florida, and a Visiting Professor at Kings College/ Guy's Hospital, University of London. He also served for 10 years as Professor of Ceramic Materials and Co-Director of the Imperial College London Tissue Engineering and Regenerative Medicine Centre and previously for 32 years as Graduate Research Professor at the University of Florida. He is a member of the U.S. National Academy of Engineering.

Hench, an Ohio native, now lives in Ft Myers, Florida.

Boing-Boing
the Bionic Cat

When Larry Hench became a grandfather, he started looking for books to read to his grandchildren that taught science concepts in a fun and interesting way, without talking down, through stories that were realistic – not fairytale-like. He couldn't find them; he was also dismayed to see scientists, professors, and engineers portrayed as evil, nutty, nerdy, absent-minded, etc... not as real, caring, helpful human beings. Larry wanted children to see the excitement and process of science, and scientists and engineers as trustworthy, interesting, and fun people. So he decided to write his own stories to accomplish these goals. Enter Boing-Boing!

Boing-Boing the Bionic Cat
978-1-904872-00-9 (Book 1)
Professor George builds a bionic cat for his young neighbor, Daniel, who is allergic to cats. To simulate behavior and characteristics of a living cat it features 8 unique designs, for example a fibre-optic fur that transmits sunlight to solar cells inside the cat to recharge its batteries.

Boing-Boing the Bionic Cat and the Jewel Thief
978-1-904872-01-6 (Book 2)
Boing-Boing's new design features, a pressure sensitive receptor in the bionic tail integrated with a voice box simulating a lion's roar, are central to a night in the Natural History Museum. Will Boing-Boing foil a cat burglar in this captivating caper?

Boing-Boing the Bionic Cat and the Lion's Claws
978-1-904872-02-3 (Book 3)

The bionic cat has new voice and color recognition programs that follow Daniel's commands to fetch red objects, such as a ball. Will a game of fetch help the dynamic duo save a little girl from the jaws of death in the the lion's pit of the London Zoo?

Boing-Boing the Bionic Cat and the Flying Trapeze
978-1-904872-05-4 (Book 4)

Professor George adds a gyroscope and an improved eye-object recognition program so that Boing-Boing can climb trees without falling. When Daniel and his friend Amy attend the circus, Boing-Boing swings into action when the suspense is too much for a trapeze artist. Will Boing-Boing fall from grace or save the day?

Boing-Boing the Bionic Cat and the Mummy's Revenge
978-1-904872-06-1 (Book 5)

An Egyptologist is trapped somewhere deep in the middle of a newly discovered pyramid built by Rameses the Great. Daniel, Professor George and Boing-Boing go to the rescue. Will the bionic cat's new infrared sensitive bionic eyes and improved voice recognition system lead them to the missing explorer?

If you have a smartphone, the QR code here will take you to exclusive online features on Boing-Boing direct from the printed page. Here's how to do it. **1.** Go online using your phone, enter 'QR code reader' into a search engine or app store. **2.** Find a compatible application for your phone. **3.** Download and install the free app. **4.** Launch the app. **5.** Activate your phone's camera. **6.** Hold the camera as if you were taking a picture of the QR code. **7.** The app will pick up the link to the web page. **8.** You should be online with Boing-Boing!

About the illustrator

The wonderful drawings in this book are by Tom Morgan-Jones. You can check out some more examples of his work and get in touch by going to **www.inkymess.com**.

Tom is an award-winning illustrator based in Cambridge, UK. He illustrates lots of things from children's books and magazines to satirical boardgames.

Tom has lectured, tutored and been an artist in residence at UK universities, colleges and schools including the Cambridge University Cartoon and Illustration Society, Cambridge School of Art and London College of Printing.

He has been awarded a D&AD (British Design and Art Direction) Yellow Pencil and a medal from the AOI (Association of Illustrators).

This is not Tom's first project with Can of Worms Kids Press. Tom is the illustrator behind the award-winning Mission:Explore series and has created his unique inky mess for three Mission:Explore titles, the iPhone App and website.

About the publisher

The Boing-Boing series is published by Can of Worms Kids Press, part of a wriggling writhing collective of book publishers run by Can of Worms Enterprises Ltd.

In addition to the Boing-Boing series, Can of Worms Kids Press also publishes the Monkey Magic and Mission:Explore series.

Monkey Magic: The Curse of Mukada
by Grant S Clark

'A beautifully written tale of good vs evil that will inspire its readers to join the fight to save the Orangutan and help save the Earth, too!" **National Geographic Kids**

Monkey Magic: The Great Wall Mystery
by Grant S Clark

"I read *Monkey Magic* to my son Robert. He loved it and is even more inspired to become a Wildlife Warrior!" **Terri Irwin, naturalist and owner of Australia Zoo**

We also do wonderful comic versions of Shakespeare's plays illustrated by more fantastic people. **www.graphicshakespeare.com**

And for those kids who have grown up or aspiring to, we have stories about ordinary people doing extraordinary things: climbing mountains, finding cannibals, cycling around the world and other amazing adventures, all published by Eye Books.

You can find out about all of our books and get special offers at **www.canofwormsenterprises.co.uk**

MISSION:EXPLORE

"Bold, cool, exciting and just plain fun!"

National Geographic

The Mission:Explore books challenge girls and boys in daring new ways. Encouraging children to draw, rub, smear, write, scrape and print their findings & achievements as they complete each mission, the books promote interaction with and exploration of the world around them.

See opposite for an example mission to try!

978-1-904872-33-7

978-1-904872-38-2

978-1-904872-41-2

"Designed to be read, scribbled on, illustrated, smeared, scratched and sniffed, it may just be the most revolutionary geography-related book ever published."

Geographical Magazine

☐ ME001
Become a pet detective

Study cats. How do they get from one place
to another? How fast can they travel? Make
a map revealing local cat routes including
symbols for danger spots, hiding places,
prey and predators.

Can you return a lost cat to its owners?

WARNING!

Do not follow cats along fence tops.

More missions and mission training can be
found at www.missionexplore.co.uk

The Boy Who Biked the World
On the Road to Africa

Alastair Humphreys
Illustrations by Tom Morgan-Jones
978-1-903070-75-8

In this charming caricature of Alastair Humphreys' infamous circumnavigation of the world on his bike, children are swept along with the character of Tom, an adventurous boy who feels there must be more to life than school!

The first part of The Boy Who Biked the World follows Tom leaving England, cycling through Europe and all the way through Africa to the tip of South Africa. Along the way, young readers are introduced not only to the various fascinating landmarks and landscapes he passes through, but also to the various people who so happily embraced him as he travelled on his journey.

With engaging illustrations, postcards and journal entries throughout, this book provides an immersive experience for any young adventurer!

Alastair Humphreys spent four years cycling round the world, a journey of 46,000 miles across five continents. His adventure is told in two books: Moods of Future Joys and Thunder & Sunshine.

Order Form for Can of Worms

Cut out and send with a cheque (payable to Can of Worms Enterprises) for the correct amount to:
7 Peacock Yard
Iliffe Street
London
SE17 3LH

OR:

E-mail us at info@canofwormsenterprises.co.uk
Call our distributors, LBS, on +44(0)1903 828500

To order online, for special offers and more information, go to our **website**: www.canofwormsenterprises.co.uk

In the **USA**, please use our distributors, Trafalgar Square.
E-mail them at orders@ipgbook.com
Or **call** them on 800.888.4741

Order Form for Can of Worms Kids Press

Fill in the number of books required in the boxes next to the titles and send to the address overleaf with a cheque. In the UK, add £2.50 P&P for the first book, with an extra 50 pence for each additional book. For the rest of the world, add £3.50/$5.50 P&P for the first book with an extra 50p/75¢ for each additional book.

No.   Title

☐ *Boing-Boing the Bionic Cat*
978-1-904872-00-9 **£4.99 UK $7.99 US**

☐ *Boing-Boing the Bionic Cat and the Jewel Thief*
978-1-904872-01-6 **£4.99 UK $7.99 US**

☐ *Boing-Boing the Bionic Cat and the Lion's Claws*
978-1-904872-02-3 **£4.99 UK $7.99 US**

☐ *Boing-Boing the Bionic Cat and the Flying Trapeze*
978-1-904872-05-4 **£4.99 UK $7.99 US**

☐ *Boing-Boing the Bionic Cat and the Mummy's Revenge*
978-1-904872-06-1 **£4.99 UK $7.99 US**

☐ *Boing-Boing the Bionic Cat and the Space Station*
978-1-904872-07-8 **£5.99 UK $8.99 US**

☐ *The Boy Who Biked the World: On the Road to Africa*
978-1-903070-75-8 **£5.99 UK $8.99 US**

☐ *Mission:Explore*
978-1-904872-33-7 **£5.99 UK $12.99 US**

☐ *Mission:Explore On the Road*
978-1-904872-38-2 **£4.99 UK $7.99 US**

☐ *Mission:Explore Camping* **£4.99**
978-1-904872-41-2 **£4.99 UK $7.99 US**

☐ *Monkey Magic: The Curse of Mukada*
978-1-904872-37-5 **£5.99 UK $8.99 US**

☐ *Monkey Magic: The Great Wall Mystery*
978-1-904872-40-5 **£5.99 UK $8.99 US**

Special discounts for schools and other offers
may be available online, please visit:
www.canofwormsenterprises.co.uk